One of my favourite things about doing events and talking to readers like you is hearing all about the animals in your lives. It could be your pet, the pet of one of your friends, or the birds you see at the park.

Whatever animals you have in your life, looking after them is a big responsibility, and, as Marv learns in this story, it doesn't always go to plan. But the important thing is that we try our best to care and look out for the creatures sharing this planet with us.

Alex

That's me!

For my cats, Akira and Simone – A.F.-K

For SUPER YOU, the completely marvellous reader – P.B.

OXFORD
UNIVERSITY PRESS

Great Clarendon Street, Oxford OX2 6DP
Oxford University Press is a department of the University of Oxford.
It furthers the University's objective of excellence in research, scholarship,
and education by publishing worldwide. Oxford is a registered trade mark
of Oxford University Press in the UK and in certain other countries

Database right Oxford University Press (maker)

First published in 2024

British Library Cataloguing in Publication Data

Data available

ISBN: 978-0-19-278052-2

1 3 5 7 9 10 8 6 4 2

Printed in China

Paper used in the production of this book is a natural,
recyclable product made from wood grown in sustainable forests.
The manufacturing process conforms to the environmental
regulations of the country of origin.

MARV

AND THE
HUMONGOUS
HAMSTER

WRITTEN BY
ALEX FALASE-KOYA

PICTURES BY
PAULA BOWLES

OXFORD
UNIVERSITY PRESS

CHAPTER 1

Marvin couldn't keep his eyes off the small rectangular cage at the front of the classroom.

A high-pitched squeak came from inside.

Marvin crept forward for a better look.

Sawdust rustled around the cage.

Marvin leaned closer, his nose almost touching the bars.

Suddenly, a fluffy creature with golden-brown fur whizzed across the cage floor.

It was Nibbles, the classroom hamster.

There was nothing like the last
day of school before the holidays. Sure,
school was fun, and Marvin loved
hanging out with his friends and seeing

his teachers, but to him, half-term was filled with a whole new set of adventures. This last day of school was even more exciting than usual, and it was all because of Nibbles.

'Who do you think it's going to be?' Joe asked, nudging Marvin. Marvin wanted to say his own name, but he didn't want to jinx it.

Ms Fry was about to announce the pupil who would be looking after Nibbles over the half-term break. Marvin desperately wanted it to be him, but with so many other kids in his class, he knew his chances were slim.

'Maybe Eva will get picked,' Marvin said.

'I'm going on holiday for some of half-term, so I can't take care of Nibbles,' Eva replied from across the room.

'I can't take Nibbles either. Dad says he's allergic,' Joe said, rolling his eyes.

Marvin looked around the room. He remembered hearing some of his classmates say that they were going on holiday too, and others that their parents wouldn't let them look after Nibbles . . . Maybe he had a chance after all?

'You think you might have a chance,' Joe said, smiling.

Marvin stared at him, shocked. It was as though Joe had read his mind. 'How did you—?'

'We're best friends—of course I know what you're thinking!'

'Reading minds *is* a best friend superpower.' Marvin rubbed his chin thoughtfully.

'Anyway, I thought you said that your grandad isn't the biggest fan of small, furry creatures—isn't that why you're not allowed a pet?' Joe said. 'What will your grandad say if Ms Fry picks you?'

'I've already spoken to Grandad about it,' Marvin said. 'He's agreed that if I get picked, we can take Nibbles home. And, if I can prove that I can look after Nibbles, then maybe Grandad will let me have a pet of my own.'

'Wait, Marvin,' came a voice from behind them. 'You don't have any pets?' It was Marv's classmate, Jasper.

'Well, no,' Marvin said quietly.

'Then there's no way that you should be the one looking after Nibbles. It should be me. I have lots of pets at home already so I'll know exactly how to take care of her,' Jasper said.

'Jasper, come on,' Joe said.

'Sorry, I'm just being truthful. I think Nibbles would be way happier in my house,' Jasper replied.

Before Marvin had a chance to think about what Jasper had said, their teacher, Ms Fry, stood at the front of the class and cleared her throat loudly.

'OK class, back in your seats, please. I've put the names of everyone who was interested in taking care of Nibbles into this hat. Are you ready for me to pick a name?'

'Yes!' replied the class.

'OK. Drum roll, please.'

The whole class began to drum on their desks as Ms Fry rummaged around in the hat. Marvin's heart trembled in his chest.

'The person looking after Nibbles over half-term is . . . Marvin!' Ms Fry announced, waving aloft a piece of paper with Marvin's name written on it.

Marvin blinked. Was it really him? Did he really get chosen?!

Joe immediately began to clap and cheer, while Jasper shot Marvin a sour look. Marvin tried to ignore it—after all, he'd won!

At home time, Marvin quickly packed up his things and bounded over to the hamster cage. 'Are you ready, Nibbles?' he asked, peering into the cage to see the hamster's little furry face looking up at him.

'Are you sure that you don't want me to take care of Nibbles? You don't want her to be miserable at your house.' Marvin turned to see Jasper watching him with a scowl on his face.

'I'm sure,' Marvin replied.

'Really? It's not like you've looked after a pet before, so how will you know what you're doing?' Jasper said.

'I'll be fine,' Marvin said, picking up the hamster cage carefully.

'It's not you I'm worried about. It's Nibbles. I bet you and Joe will be too busy having fun over half-term to even play with her. I bet you abandon her the minute you get bored.'

Marvin ignored Jasper and carried the cage out of the classroom and across the playground. Even though Marvin knew what Jasper said wasn't right, he couldn't help thinking about it. Marvin was determined to prove Jasper wrong!

Marvin's grandad met him at the school gate. He sighed when he noticed Marvin carefully carrying Nibbles' cage in his arms.

'OK, Marvin, this is your chance to show me how responsible you can be,' Grandad said. 'You are responsible for looking after Nibbles, including cleaning out her cage and replacing her food and water.'

'I promise I'll be responsible. You won't regret it,' Marvin said.

That evening before bed, Marvin set up the hamster cage on his bedside table and took Nibbles out to give her a tour of his room.

Marvin held Nibbles carefully in his hands and carried her over to the wardrobe.

'Here's my wardrobe, Nibbles.' Marvin opened his wardrobe door and pointed at a blue superhero costume with a large 'M' emblazoned on the chest. 'And this is my super-suit,' Marvin declared. 'When supervillains strike, and people need help, I put on my super-suit and become a superhero called Marv.' Nibbles seemed to nod her head, or at least that's what Marvin thought she was doing—it was hard to tell. 'You'll have to keep my real identity a secret, though. No one knows I'm a superhero, apart from Grandad.'

'And me! Hello, I'm Pixel.' A robotic voice came from the top of Marvin's bookcase.

Pixel—a small, round, silvery robot—whirred to life and hovered down from the bookcase towards Marvin and Nibbles.

'I'm Marvin's sidekick. I come along on all his superhero adventures and help him out,' Pixel said. She leaned in towards Marvin. 'Do you think Nibbles understands what we're saying?'

'Of course she does! Nibbles is super smart,' Marvin nodded as he took Nibbles back to her cage.

'But that's where I usually sleep,' said Pixel, pointing to the bedside table.

'I know. I'm sorry, Pixel, but I need to keep Nibbles close to my bed so I can keep an eye on her and get her anything she needs in the night. Is it OK if you sleep somewhere else? It's just for tonight, while Nibbles settles in.'

'OK,' Pixel replied sadly, settling back down on the bookshelf.

'See, there's plenty of space for everyone,' Marvin said, turning out the light and getting into bed. He snuggled down under the covers, suddenly feeling very tired after the day's excitement. 'Goodnight, Nibbles,' he said with a yawn.

'Goodnight, Marvin,' whispered Pixel, but Marvin was already fast asleep.

CHAPTER 2

DING DONG!

Marvin rushed downstairs to get the door, leaping over the last two steps. It was the first day of the holidays and Joe and Eva were coming over to see Nibbles.

'Hey!' Marvin said as he opened his front door.

'Hey, Marvin,' Eva waved.

'Where's Nibbles? I have to see Nibbles!' Joe cried out, barging past Eva and Marvin into the house.

They went up to Marvin's room and
stood in front of Nibbles' cage, staring at
the tiny hamster.

'You know what?' Joe said. 'I
think Nibbles could use a little bit of
excitement.'

'That's a good idea,' said Marv. 'What shall we do?'

'We could all dress up as hamsters! I'm sure Nibbles would find it really exciting if we were all giant hamsters.'

Eva looked thoughtful. 'I think she'd find that scary. Imagine if you woke up one day and there were giant people everywhere.'

Marvin and Joe nodded.

'I had another idea,' Marvin said. 'What if we made something like this?' Marvin opened his sketchbook and showed his friends.

Marvin, Joe, and Eva searched the house high and low for used toilet rolls, scissors, tape and empty delivery boxes.

Once they'd gathered the materials
they needed, the friends got to work, and
in no time at all, their masterpiece was
complete.

The team stood back and admired
their handiwork.

'What do you think?' Eva asked.

'I think it's perfect,' Marvin replied.

Cardboard boxes and loo rolls had been cut up and arranged into a giant hamster maze that took up Marvin's whole bedroom floor.

'Now, we're just missing a hamster.'
Marvin grinned at his friends.

They let Nibbles out of her cage, sat
her down in the centre of the maze, and
then Nibbles was off!

They didn't even have to
put hamster treats down to
guide her.

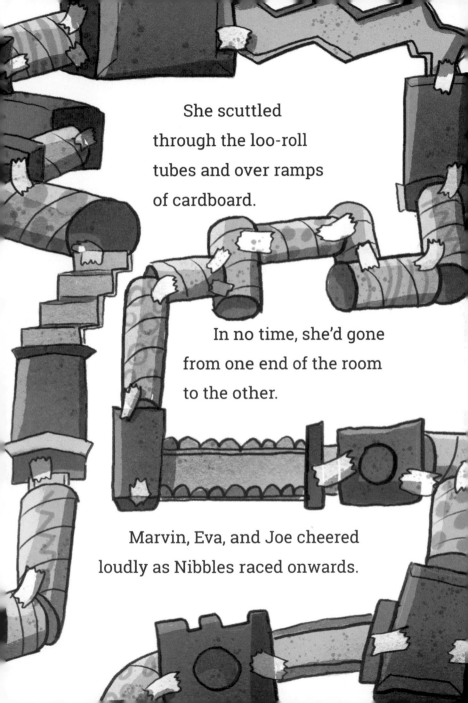

She scuttled
through the loo-roll
tubes and over ramps
of cardboard.

In no time, she'd gone
from one end of the room
to the other.

Marvin, Eva, and Joe cheered
loudly as Nibbles raced onwards.

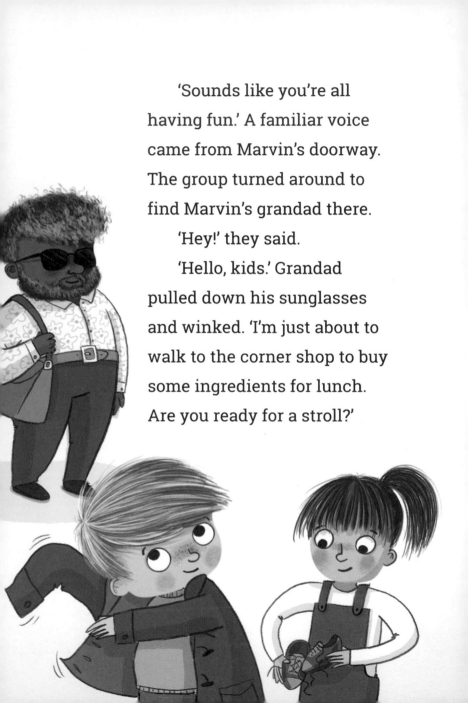

'Sounds like you're all having fun.' A familiar voice came from Marvin's doorway. The group turned around to find Marvin's grandad there.

'Hey!' they said.

'Hello, kids.' Grandad pulled down his sunglasses and winked. 'I'm just about to walk to the corner shop to buy some ingredients for lunch. Are you ready for a stroll?'

'I like walks. Let's go,' Marvin said. Secretly, he was hoping he could persuade his grandad to buy them some sweets from the shop.

Marvin, Joe, and Eva put their shoes on and got ready to leave the house, but as Marvin was about to put Nibbles back into her cage, he started to worry. What if Nibbles got lonely being left all on her own? Marvin could hear Jasper's words in his head again.

Are you sure that you don't want me to take care of Nibbles? You don't want her to be miserable at your house.

What would someone who was doing a really good job of looking after Nibbles do? Marvin didn't want her to be lonely . . .

Marvin turned to Eva and Joe. 'Go on ahead. I just need to do something quickly.' The moment they were gone, Marvin put Nibbles in his pocket with a few small pieces of cucumber to keep her happy.

The whirring sound of a small robot waking up made Marvin turn around. Pixel rose from the bookshelf.

'What about me? Can't I come too?' she asked, with a sad frown.

'Sure,' Marvin said. 'You never know when adventure will strike. That's what Grandad always says.'

Marvin popped Pixel and his super-suit in his backpack and took the bag with him as he left the house.

Grandad led the way down the road to the corner shop. It didn't take long for them to get there. On the other side of the road, opposite the corner shop, was a huge playground. Immediately, Joe and Eva's eyes were glued to it, but Marvin was keen to get back home.

'We can stop and have a play if you want?' Grandad said.

'Yes, please,' Eva and Joe said

without hesitating. Marvin was quiet. Nibbles was wriggling in his pocket, and it was getting hard for him to keep her from popping out. He couldn't lose her.

'Maybe we should skip the playground today,' Marvin said, while he stroked Nibbles in his pocket, trying to keep her still.

Grandad rested a hand on Marvin's shoulder. 'I know you want to get back and see Nibbles, but she won't mind if you and your friends have fun at the park for a few minutes.'

'Come on, Marvin. Pleeease?' pleaded Joe.

'OK,' agreed Marvin. 'Just for a few minutes though.'

They crossed the road
to the park and ran toward
the swings, but soon
stopped, noticing someone
was already there. A boy
was standing on top of the
swings frame. It looked
dangerous. Marvin had no
idea how he could have got
up there.

The boy was around Marvin's age and was wearing a super-suit with weird symbols on it—they looked a bit like the coding and maths symbols Marvin used at school. The boy also had a utility belt with scientific equipment on it, from test tubes and goggles to high-tech gadgets. It looked as though the boy was carrying around an entire science lab—but the thing that alarmed Marvin the most was the huge blaster ray in the boy's hand.

The boy turned slightly and noticed Marvin and his grandad and friends, watching him.

'This is perfect—an audience for my first experiment,' the boy said.

'Oh no, not another supervillain,' Joe said, going very pale. 'Why do they always appear when I'm around?'

Marvin knew that Joe was right—the boy was a supervillain, and he looked dangerous.

'My name is Dr Boom, and I'm here to test out my latest invention. Mwah-ha-ha-ha!' Dr Boom cackled.

Nibbles wriggled hard in Marvin's pocket. She was probably allergic to supervillains, as all good hamsters are.

'It's the playground today and world domination tomorrow!' Dr Boom continued. Then he lifted the blaster ray and pointed it down at the playground below.

This is not good, thought Marvin, but, before he could react, Dr Boom pressed a button on the blaster ray and then . . .

BOOOOOOOOOOM!

CHAPTER 3

A bolt of electricity rocketed out of Dr Boom's blaster ray and struck the playground slide. It wobbled and vibrated, and then with a POP, it shrunk to the size of a shoe! The slide was so small now that, if Marvin wanted to, he could pick it up with one hand.

'Yes! My invention works!' Dr Boom cackled. Then he turned a dial on the blaster ray, pointed it at a see-saw, and fired again.

BOOOOOOOOOM!

The see-saw wobbled and
vibrated, and then with a POP, instead
of shrinking, the see-saw exploded
upwards. It was ten times bigger than it
was before.

Marvin heard a scream, and he whipped around to see a couple of families dive into some nearby bushes. They must have been terrified! And they weren't the only ones.

Nibbles wriggled out of Marvin's
pocket and jumped to the ground before
making a dash across the playground.
'Nibbles, NOOO!' shouted Marvin.

A mischievous grin spread across Dr Boom's face. 'Ah, perfect!' he said, pointing his blaster ray at Nibbles and blasting her just before she disappeared into the bushes.

Marvin gasped. What setting was the blaster on? Would Nibbles be big, or would she somehow get even smaller?

How would he ever find her if that happened?

The bushes shook back and forth. There was an earth-shaking sound, like a lion roaring. Then out of the bushes crashed Nibbles. She was ENORMOUS. At least the size of a hippo. The ground sunk beneath her heavy feet.

'MARVIN!' Grandad cried. 'Why on earth did you bring Nibbles?'

Marvin opened his mouth, but nothing came out—he didn't know what to say.

'Well, Joe, it looks like we have a giant hamster after all, just like you wanted.' Eva laughed nervously.

'I said we should dress up like hamsters, not that Nibbles should be supersized!' Joe cried, pointing at Nibbles. She was standing in the middle of the playground. Her head darted from side to side nervously. Marvin wanted to scoop her up and cuddle her, but she was far too big.

There was only one way to stop all this, and Marvin knew exactly what he had to do. He just needed to create a distraction. Marvin glanced over to his grandad, who gave a small nod of his head.

Grandad stepped forward, getting closer to the swing and Dr Boom.

'So, er . . . what type of power source are you using for your blaster ray invention?' he asked.

'Oh,' Dr Boom glanced down with a grin. 'I'm using a hydrogen-powered fuel cell, combined with a solar-powered backup. How much do you know about portable energy sources?'

'Erm, not much,' Grandad said, with a confused look on his face.

'Great! That means I get to tell you all about how smart I am!' said Dr Boom. He began a lengthy speech about his inventions. Now was Marvin's chance. He turned to Joe and Eva.

'I'm going to sneak off and get some help,' Marvin whispered.

'We could really do with a superhero, so if you know any, now would be a good time to get them,' Joe replied.

'Yeah, I don't want to be made really big or really tiny. I'm happy as I am,' Eva said.

'Trust me. I'll be back as soon as I can,' Marvin replied, running off.

As soon as he was out of sight, Marvin dived behind a bush and opened his backpack. Pixel popped out.

'Where was the usual "Supervillain detected!" alarm?' Marvin asked.

'I think it's pretty obvious that this boy is a supervillain, so I saved my energy for this instead,' Pixel replied, doing a little dance in the air.

Marvin nodded. 'That is cool, but we have a supervillain to stop.'

Marvin pulled his super-suit out of the backpack and threw it on. He was now MARV, the superhero!

Marv and Pixel made their way back to the playground.

'Is that a superhero I see?' Dr Boom immediately noticed Marv and Pixel's arrival. 'Well, get ready to be super tiny!' he yelled, pointing his blaster ray straight at Marv.

BOOOOOOOOOOOOM!

The electricity bolt headed straight towards Marv, but at the last second Grandad leapt in the way. He stood for a moment seeming perfectly fine, but then the blaster ray's power began to take effect. Marv's grandad wobbled and vibrated, and then with a POP, Grandad shrunk to the size of a mouse!

CHAPTER 4

Dr Boom aimed the blaster ray at Marv again.

'Super-suit, please activate sonic blast,' Marv whispered quickly, with one hand pressed to the 'M' on his chest.

Marv pushed both arms forward. A wave of air rippled from the palms of his hands, rushing towards Dr Boom, knocking him off the swings and to the ground.

As Dr Boom lay dazed on the floor, Marv ran over to Grandad and gently picked him up.

'Grand . . . ahem, I mean, member of the public . . . are you OK?' Marv said.

'Don't you worry about me,' said Grandad in a squeaky voice. 'Hand me to Joe and Eva—you have to stop this dastardly supervillain!'

Marv passed Grandad to Joe and Eva and turned to face Dr Boom, but Dr Boom wasn't on the ground any more! He had climbed on top of Nibbles' back and was using a rope from his tool belt as a harness.

Nibbles reared up on her hind legs and shook out her fur.

'Woah!' Marv said. Nibbles looked like the most majestic creature he had ever seen!

'OK, it's time to stop pooping all over the playground, hamster. We need to gallop over to the pet shop,' Dr Boom said. 'I think it'll be fun to try my new invention on some more animals. Imagine rats, mice, guinea pigs, and rabbits once I've made them all the size of elephants, rhinos, and hippos. My army of animals will be unstoppable!'

'No, it won't! How are you going to get all those animals to do what you want?' Marv asked.

'It's pretty easy, actually,' Dr Boom said, and then he turned to Nibbles. 'Come with me, and you can have all the carrots you can stuff inside those massive cheeks of yours.'

Nibbles immediately nodded at
Dr Boom. She pawed the ground like a
horse preparing to stampede. Mud and
dust were kicked up from the floor all
over the place. Then Nibbles let out an
almighty roar and galloped away from the
playground.

Marv knew he had to stop Dr Boom
and fast!

'Super-suit, please activate rocket boosters!' Marv said. The suit crackled, and then a set of rocket boosters emerged from Marv's back and blasted

into action. Marv grabbed Pixel and
together they rocketed through the air.

'Woohoo!' Marv yelled as
the wind rushed past him.

'Nibbles seems like a bad hamster to me. You know, I'd never join a supervillain so easily. According to my calculations, there's a 99.99 per cent chance I'd say no,' Pixel shouted over the sound of the rocket boosters. Marv couldn't understand why Pixel was being so harsh about Nibbles. None of this was really her fault.

'Hey, Pixel. Were you feeling jealous of Nibbles earlier—'

Pixel didn't get a chance to answer.

Ahead of them, Dr Boom had begun to blast the parked cars in his way, making them look like tiny, toy cars.

'Sorry, cars! I'll turn you all back to normal later!' Marv yelled as he zoomed past.

Dr Boom and Nibbles rampaged onwards. They turned a corner, and Marv and Pixel lost sight of them. Nibbles could really move!

BOOOOOOOM!

Marv zoomed up into the air, flying higher and higher until he could see Nibbles down below. She was outside a fruit and vegetable shop. Marv swooped down and landed on the pavement next to her.

There was a huge, well-ordered display of fruit and vegetables outside the front of the shop, though it didn't look like it would be there for much longer. Nibbles was happily chomping her way through the entire display, stuffing cauliflowers, carrots, apples, and pears into her cheek pouches.

Her cheeks were really BULGING!

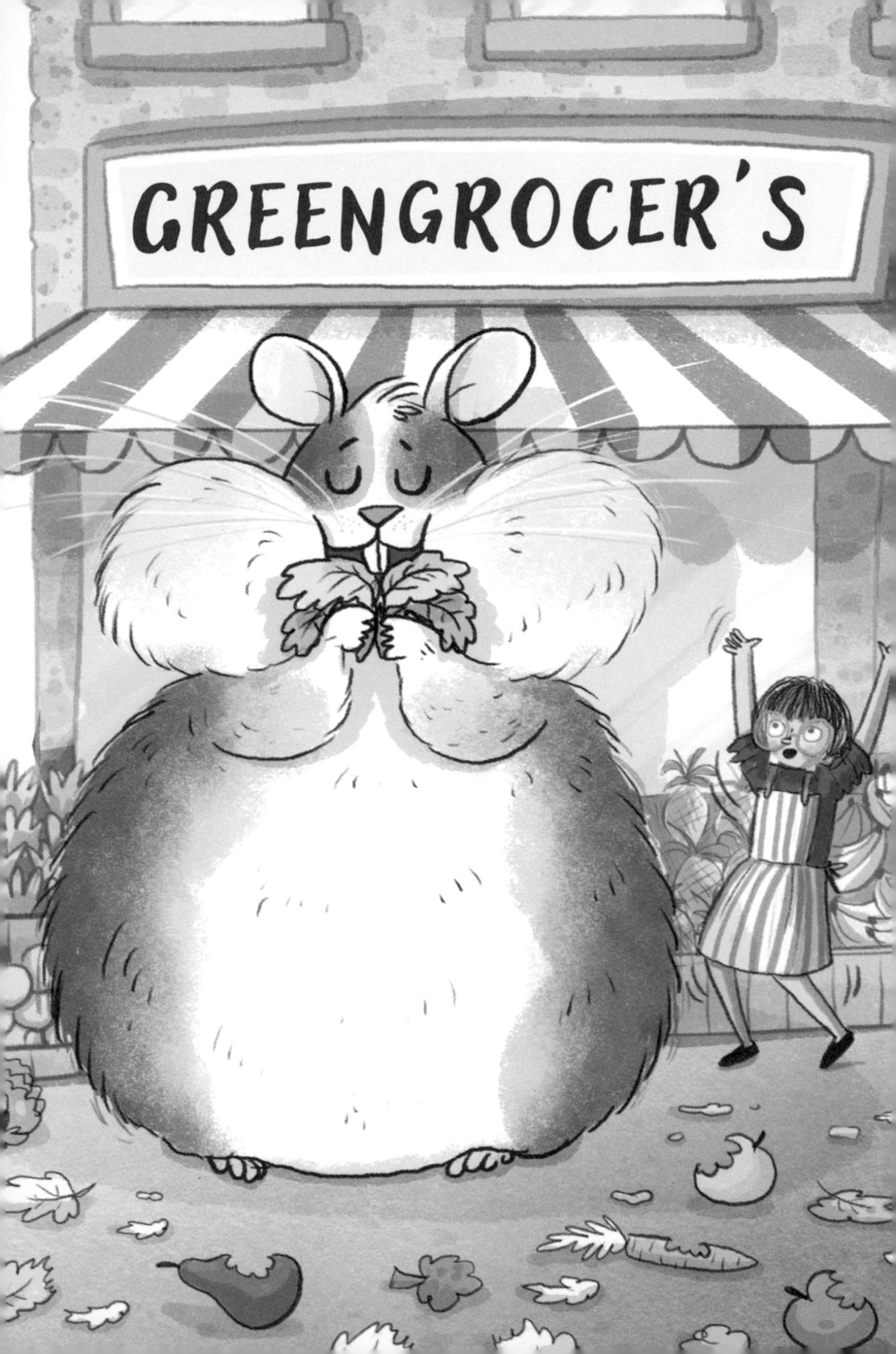
GREENGROCER'S

But where was Dr Boom?

A flustered-looking shopkeeper saw Marv and quickly pointed down the street. 'If you're looking for the supervillain, he went that way. He needs to come and collect this furry beast—look at all this mess!'

'Thank you,' replied Marv. 'We'll be back to get Nibbles soon, I promise.' Marv hoped that the hamster wouldn't cause too much trouble while they dealt with Dr Boom.

Marv and Pixel zoomed after Dr Boom. They soon caught up with him, but before they could confront the supervillain, he reached into his utility belt, plucked out a bottle of liquid, and threw it on the ground behind him.

The instant the bottle smashed on to the floor, a thick, heavy mist wafted into the air, and Marv and Pixel could no longer see where they were going.

'I'll take care of this with my super-sidekick fan hands!' Pixel said. Her hands spun around at super-speed until her fingers acted like the blades of a fan. They blew away the mist to reveal Dr Boom disappearing into a pet shop at the end of the street.

'Quick! We have to stop him before he uses his blaster ray on the animals,' Marv shouted.

CHAPTER 5

'Somebody, help! There's a supervillain in my pet shop!' the owner cried as she came running out of the store.

'We'll stop him!' Marv said. He and Pixel zoomed past the shopkeeper and into the shop. Dr Boom had worked fast. The place was already bursting at the seams with giant rats, hamsters, and rabbits! They rampaged through the shop, chomping through the pet food on the shelves, and leaving humongous poos everywhere. They looked as though they were having the time of their lives, but they were causing an awful mess.

Through the crowd of enormous furry animals, Marv spotted Dr Boom. He was pressed up against a shelf, trying to make himself look as small as possible. He looked a little bit afraid. Nibbles was

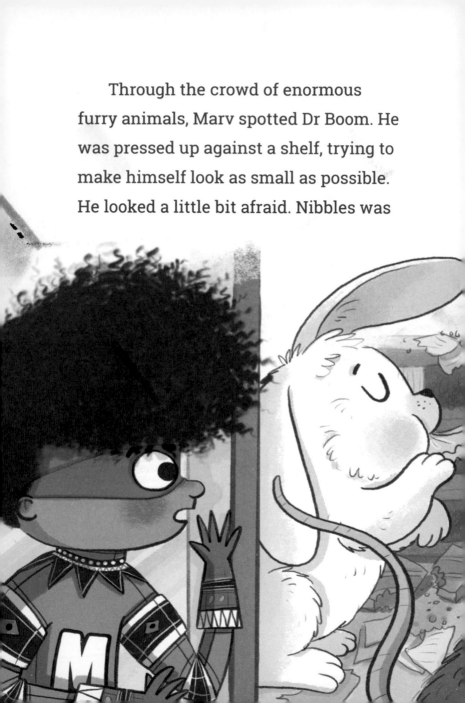

just one massive hamster—Dr Boom
could deal with that—but now he was
surrounded by loads of super-sized pets,
and it looked as though it was too much
for him.

'Argh!' Dr Boom shouted, as he dived out of the way of a bunny thumping through the shop with its big, heavy paws. 'I need to make them small again!' Dr Boom began frantically fiddling with the dial on his blaster ray, but he was so nervous that he couldn't get it set right. 'It's no use! I've got to get out of here!' he cried, making a run for the exit.

Marv and Pixel ran towards Dr Boom, ducking and diving out of the way of the massive creatures crashing into shelves and sending cages tumbling to the ground. Dr Boom's path was blocked by the giant animals. 'Argh!' he yelped as a giant guinea pig lowered its head towards him. The creature's nose twitched as it sniffed him up and down. Dr Boom leapt back in fright, dropping his blaster on to the floor. With a great big **BOOOOOOOM** the blaster accidentally went off—and it was pointing right at Marv and Pixel!

Marv didn't stop to think. He reached out and pushed Pixel out of the way, but he couldn't save himself. The electric bolt blasted into him.

Suddenly, Marv started to feel
funny. He shut his eyes tight. He
wobbled and vibrated, and then . . .
Marv opened his eyes and looked
around. The pet shop seemed dark and
shadowy all of a sudden. There was this
big silver moon above him.

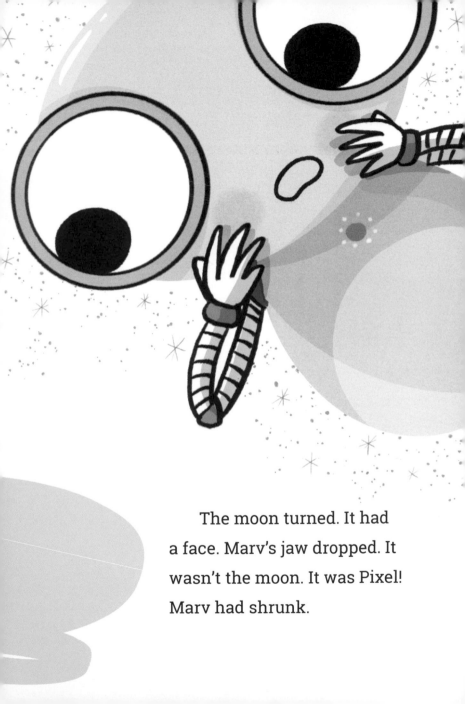

The moon turned. It had
a face. Marv's jaw dropped. It
wasn't the moon. It was Pixel!
Marv had shrunk.

Marv was now the size of a tiny mouse, and the gigantic animals running riot around the pet shop seemed even scarier than they had been before.

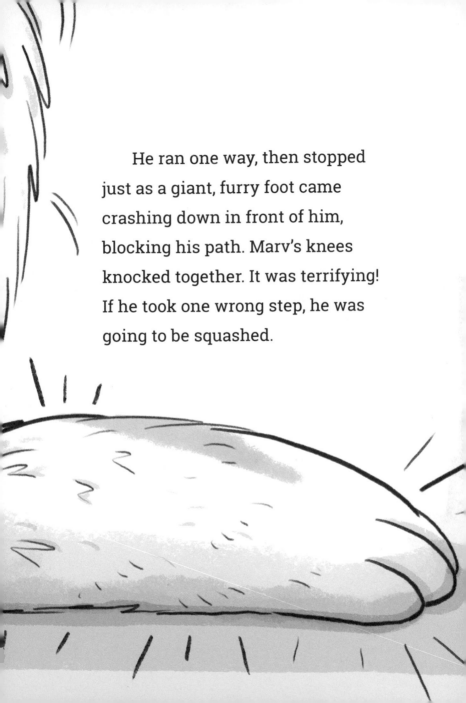

He ran one way, then stopped just as a giant, furry foot came crashing down in front of him, blocking his path. Marv's knees knocked together. It was terrifying! If he took one wrong step, he was going to be squashed.

Marv could see a high shelf still upright on the other side of the pet shop. Maybe he could be safe up there, out of the way of the animals? He just had to get over there. Marv took a deep breath. He might be tiny, but he was still a superhero. He could do this!

Marv activated his rocket boosters and flew across the pet shop as fast as he could, dodging all of the animals and landing on the shelf.

From up on the shelf, Marv could see the entire shop below him. The huge furry creatures were on the move, nibbling at food and clattering into shelves and shop displays. In the middle of the chaos were Pixel and Dr Boom, and on the floor between them was the blaster.

Marv watched as Pixel charged towards the blaster and scooped it up off the floor before Dr Boom could get his hands on it. She quickly turned the dial and aimed the ray straight at Marv.

BOOM!

When the bolt hit Marv, he felt the same odd feeling. He began to wobble and vibrate, and then—POP! Marv looked around—he was back to his normal size.

'Whew! Thanks, Pixel. Being tiny was not fun,' Marv said, jumping down from the shelf.

'As your sidekick, it is my duty to never let anyone squish you!' Pixel replied.

'You just wait!' came a shout from across the shop.

Marv and Pixel turned to watch as Dr Boom slowly walked backwards towards the exit.

'I'll be back, with loads of new inventions to try out!' Dr Boom roared. 'But for now, I'm going to run away . . . and don't even think about following me.'

Dr Boom ran for the exit, nervously glancing around at the giant animals as he went.

'Should we go after him?' Pixel asked. 'I'm still annoyed that he shrunk you.'

'No, we have a lot of work to do right here first,' Marv replied. Giant animals were still stomping through the pet shop, and the place was a complete mess.

This was a job for a superhero!

CHAPTER 6

Pixel started tidying up, while Marv used the blaster ray to turn the pets back to their normal size. They seemed a little sad not to be huge any more, but they were very full and ready for a nap after eating almost all the pet food in the shop, so they were happy for Marv to settle them back into their cages.

Pixel fetched the worried pet shop owner from outside. She hurried round the shop to check on the animals, before rushing over to Marv and Pixel.

'Thank you so much. You saved my
shop!' she said, shaking Marv and Pixel
by the hand.

With the pet shop situation under control, Marv and Pixel decided it was time to go and fix the rest of Dr Boom's mess.

'Come on, Pixel! We need to get Nibbles.' Marv reactivated his rocket boosters, and they flew through the streets, blasting the cars back to their usual sizes along the way.

'Thanks for pushing me out of the way of the blaster ray,' Pixel said.

'It was no biggie,' Marv replied. 'You're the best sidekick anyone could ever ask for. I would do anything to help my sidekick—to help my friend.' Marv smiled at Pixel.

'Even becoming really small and risking being pooped on or squashed?' Pixel grinned.

'Even that,' Marv laughed. 'I just wish I could have been as good a friend to Nibbles. I put her in danger today.' Marv's face fell.

'Don't worry. I'm sure she's still at the fruit and veg shop waiting for us. And if not, we can find her, together.'

The dynamic duo high-fived each other in mid-air and sped towards the greengrocer's. As they got closer, they heard a loud, low rumbling sound. Marv and Pixel turned to each other with eyebrows raised.

On the ground outside the fruit and veg shop was a nest of ripped-up cardboard boxes, and on top of the nest was Nibbles. She was snoring loudly.

It was no wonder she was exhausted. It had been quite the day!

The owner of the fruit and veg shop, as well as the customers, had been taking care of Nibbles while Marv and Pixel were gone. The hamster was awfully big but still awfully cute—so cute that customers had been queueing up to give Nibbles a little cuddle.

Marv asked everyone to stand back
and then used the blaster ray to turn
Nibbles back to her regular size.

He gently scooped Nibbles into his hands. 'Super-suit, please activate super-comfortable hamster pouch,' Marv whispered. A fluffy hamster pouch popped out of the side of Marv's waistband, and he carefully put Nibbles in there.

On their way back to the playground, Marv turned all the shrunken things back to their normal sizes.

At the park entrance, Joe and Eva were anxiously waiting for Marv. Joe was holding Grandad carefully in the palm of his hand.

'Have no fear! Dr Boom has been defeated, and we've undone all his experiments ... well, almost all of them,'

Marv said, looking at his tiny grandad.

'That's really good to hear, Marv. I've had enough experiments for a lifetime I think,' Grandad replied in his squeaky voice.

'Yeah, I don't know what I would have told my friend Marvin if his grandad had to stay tiny forever,' Joe said.

'A tiny grandad is not ideal. Glad to help,' Marv said.

Marv used Dr Boom's blaster ray to return his grandad, the slide, and the see-saw back to their normal sizes. Marv handed the blaster ray to Grandad.

'You seem like a trustworthy adult. I'm sure you'll be able to properly dispose of this,' Marv nodded.

'Of course,' Grandad nodded back.

Lastly, Marv carefully lifted Nibbles out of the pouch by his suit. 'I believe this belongs to Marvin,' he said.

He handed the hamster over to Eva. 'Thank you for your help, kind citizens. I'll see you next time!' Marv waved and then rushed away from the playground, with Pixel following close behind. He found the bush with his clothes stashed under it and got changed. Pixel and his super-suit went back into his backpack.

He was no longer Marv—he was Marvin!

Five minutes later, Marvin rushed back over to the playground. 'Where have you been?' Eva asked as he approached.

'I was looking for help, and then I bumped into Marv. He looked like he was on the case, so I made my way back here. I was a little out of breath, so it took me a while to get back,' Marvin said.

'You missed Marv again! He defeated Dr Boom!' Joe cried.

'Ah, that sounds so exciting. I'm sad I missed it,' Marvin shrugged. 'But I'm glad that everyone is safe and sound.'

The group finally began to walk back home—after buying some lunch, of course!

'I'm really, really sorry for bringing

Nibbles to the park,' said Marvin. 'I didn't want her to be lonely at home, and I didn't think about how things could have gone wrong.' Marvin sighed. 'I know I need to do more than just tell you that I can be trusted to look after Nibbles—I need to earn your trust by showing you I can take care of her.'

'That's right,' Grandad nodded and smiled. 'Luckily, we're only on day one of the holidays and there's plenty of time to show me how well you can care for a pet.'

Marvin smiled back.

'Right,' he said.

ABOUT THE AUTHOR

ALEX FALASE-KOYA

Alex is a London native. He has been writing
children's fiction since he was a teenager
and was a winner of Spread the Word's 2019
London Writers Awards for YA and Children's.
He co-wrote *The Breakfast Club Adventures*,
the first fiction book by Marcus Rashford.
He now lives in Walthamstow with his
girlfriend and two cats.

ABOUT THE ILLUSTRATOR

PAULA BOWLES

Paula grew up in Hertfordshire, and has
always loved drawing, reading, and using
her imagination, so she studied illustration
at Falmouth College of Arts and became an
illustrator. She now lives in Weston-super-Mare,
and has worked as an illustrator for over ten
years. She has had books published with Nosy
Crow and Simon & Schuster.

MARV

Marvin's life changed when he found an old superhero suit and became MARV. The suit has been passed down through Marvin's family and was last worn by his grandad. It's powered by the kindness and imagination of the wearer and doesn't work for just anybody.

COURAGE	7
FRIENDSHIP	9
KINDNESS	9
POWERS	10
AGILITY	7
COMBAT SKILLS	6

PIXEL

PIXEL is Marv's brave superhero sidekick. Her quick thinking and unwavering loyalty make her the perfect crime-fighting companion.

COURAGE	6
FRIENDSHIP	10
KINDNESS	9
POWERS	5
AGILITY	7
COMBAT SKILLS	5

DR BOOM

DR BOOM loves maths, science, coding, and inventing. Creating and testing new inventions are his favourite things to do, even if they cause trouble!

COURAGE	4
FRIENDSHIP	6
KINDNESS	5
POWERS	7
AGILITY	7
COMBAT SKILLS	6

'THE SUPER-SUIT IS POWERED BY TWO THINGS: **KINDNESS** AND **IMAGINATION**. LUCKILY YOU, MARVIN, HAVE TONS OF BOTH!'

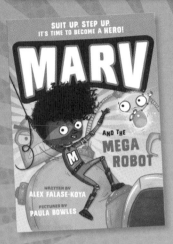

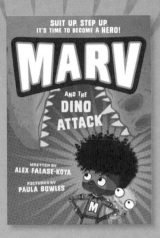

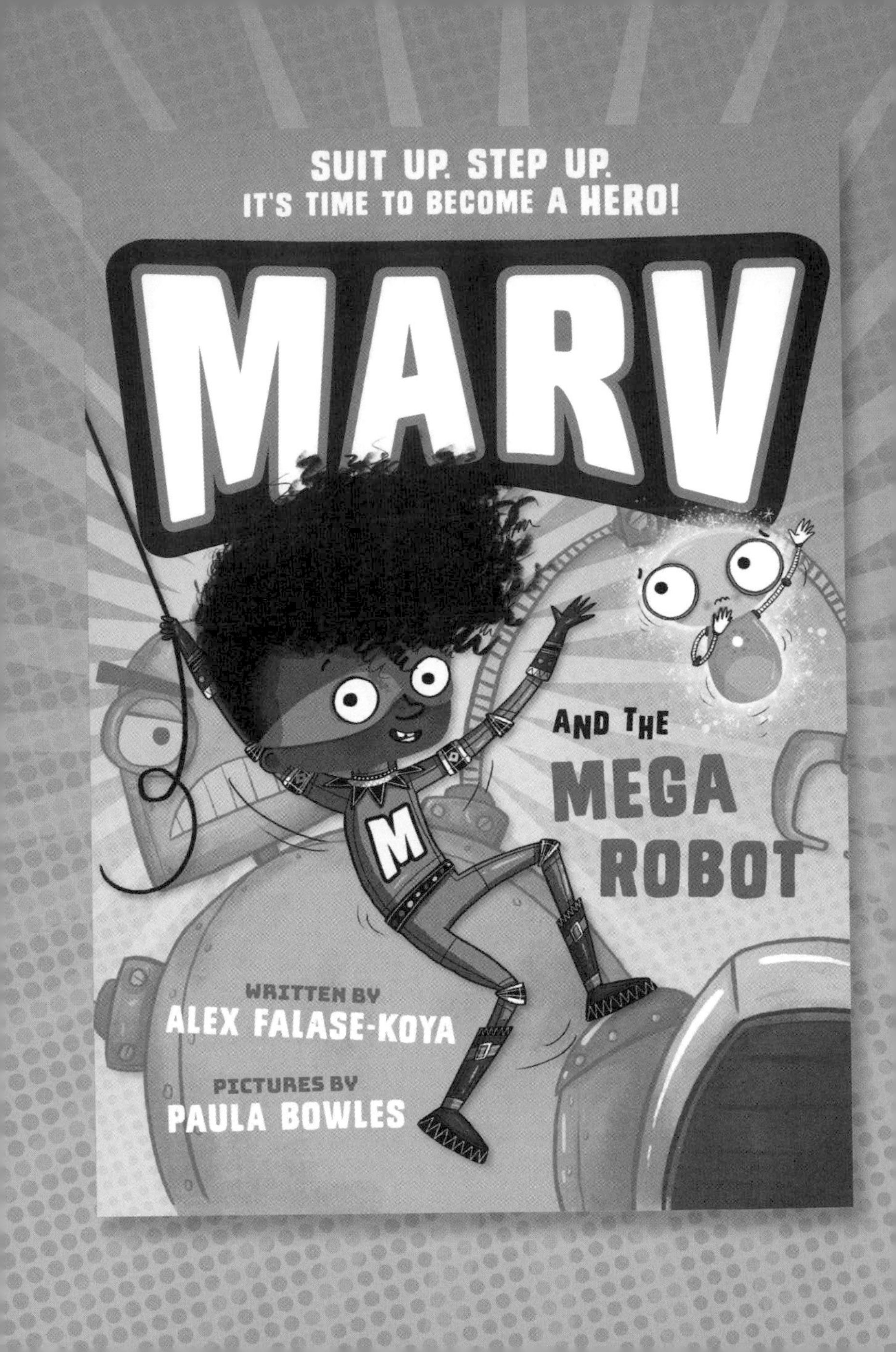
SUIT UP. STEP UP.
IT'S TIME TO BECOME A HERO!
MARV
AND THE
MEGA
ROBOT
M
WRITTEN BY
ALEX FALASE-KOYA
PICTURES BY
PAULA BOWLES

SUIT UP. STEP UP.
IT'S TIME TO BECOME A **HERO!**

Marvin loves reading about superheroes, and now he's about to become one for real.

Grandad is passing his superhero suit and robot sidekick, Pixel, on to Marvin. It's been a long time since the world needed a superhero but now, with a mega robot and a supervillain on the loose, that time has come.

To defeat his enemies and protect his friends, Marvin must learn to trust the superhero within. Only then will Marvin become MARV——unstoppable, invincible, and **totally marvellous!**

'THE SUPER-SUIT IS POWERED BY TWO THINGS:
KINDNESS AND **IMAGINATION**.
LUCKILY YOU, MARVIN, HAVE TONS OF BOTH!'

Marvin is on a school trip to the dinosaur museum when supervillain Rex makes the dinosaur skeletons come alive. He wants one for a sidekick and he wants it NOW!

When Marvin puts on his superhero suit he becomes MARV—unstoppable, invincible and totally marvellous. Chased through the museum by a rampaging T-Rex and then surrounded by velociraptors, Marv must use the power of his suit to save the day.

Marv and Pixel are about to show Rex that you can't make someone be your sidekick—you need to earn their respect and friendship first.

SUIT UP. STEP UP.
IT'S TIME TO BECOME A HERO!

MARV

AND THE
DINO
ATTACK

WRITTEN BY
ALEX FALASE-KOYA

PICTURES BY
PAULA BOWLES

LOVE MARV?
WHY NOT TRY THESE TOO...?

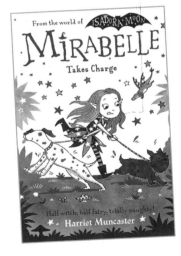